I0788149

Old Farmer John Had a Farm

By: Glenn Mosby

Disclaimer Copyright © Year 2024
All Rights Reserved
ISBN
Kindle: 978-1-964365-17-6
Paperback: 978-1-964365-18-3
Hardback: 978-1-964365-19-0

Dedication

I dedicate the children's book, Old Farmer John Had A Farm to my youngest grandkids; Mahogani, Marquis Jr., Truth, Melody and Kassh. You along with the rest of my older grandkids; Calique, Onye and Anthony Jr. are all important pieces of my heart. Each child and each piece are different in their own ways but each piece is important the same way.

To Mahogani, Marquis Jr, Truth and Kassh; I hope you find greatness in everything you do and that you find great enjoyment in reading this book or having it read to you. And always remember PaPa loves you.

Acknowledgment

I would like to acknowledge my mother; Jane Mosby. Not only was she a great mother, grandmother and great grandmother; she was also a good woman, a Christian woman and the strongest woman I knew. She lived to be 85 years old, a widow for 24 years, survived lung cancer and half her leg amputated before surrendering to heart failure. Her heart may have given out but her soul still lives in me. She was also great in spoken poetry. She would be the first one the churches would call when they wanted or needed someone on their program to add that pizzazz; that is right on point but makes you laugh. She was the best to ever do it. Everyone called her Ms. Janie, but I called her Mama. I love you Mama; and I miss you. I acknowledge you, and for all you have done. You are part of me and who I am. Without you none of this could've been possible.

About the Author

I was born Glenn Ellery Mosby, the youngest of 3 siblings born and raised in the Southside of Richmond VA to George and Jane Mosby. I grew up and fell in love with the game of baseball. I played from the age 9 in Little League thru the age of 19 in high school and American Legion. I graduated high school with a trade in Commercial Arts before going on to work for the U.S. Postal service at the age of 21. I retired early from the US Postal service on disability after 11 years. I then volunteered in my son's elementary school for 5 years. There I became coach, program coordinator, supervisor and instructor of the Before and After school program for 3 years. During my son's 5th grade year I wrote and helped produced a movie for the kindergartens thru 2nd grade. I used two 5th graders for certain roles. One happened to be my son. I resigned from Richmond Public Schools and started my own small businesses. First I started an school van transportation service for out of school zone students who required their own transportation to school. Then I started an AAU Basketball program for at risk and underrated players to be able to compete with some of the best of the best players in the country and get the experience of traveling and playing against them. When the economy took that big hit and people were losing their homes I stopped doing such business. As time and circumstances changed; so too did these things. Due to things I had no control of; I would concentrate only on those things I could change. I think that is called serenity; to accept the things you cannot change and have the courage to change the things you can. But, have the wisdom to know the difference.

From the time I was able to write; I knew it was something I loved to do. I grew up watching my mama in church recite poetry in a way that I had never seen before. She had a way with words; and a way to say them. I admired this talent. I would later on recognize this talent for writing; this talent for poetry; this talent for storytelling that I had. So I've used those talents combined with my mama's wit for humorous poetic skits. My tale is just beginning.

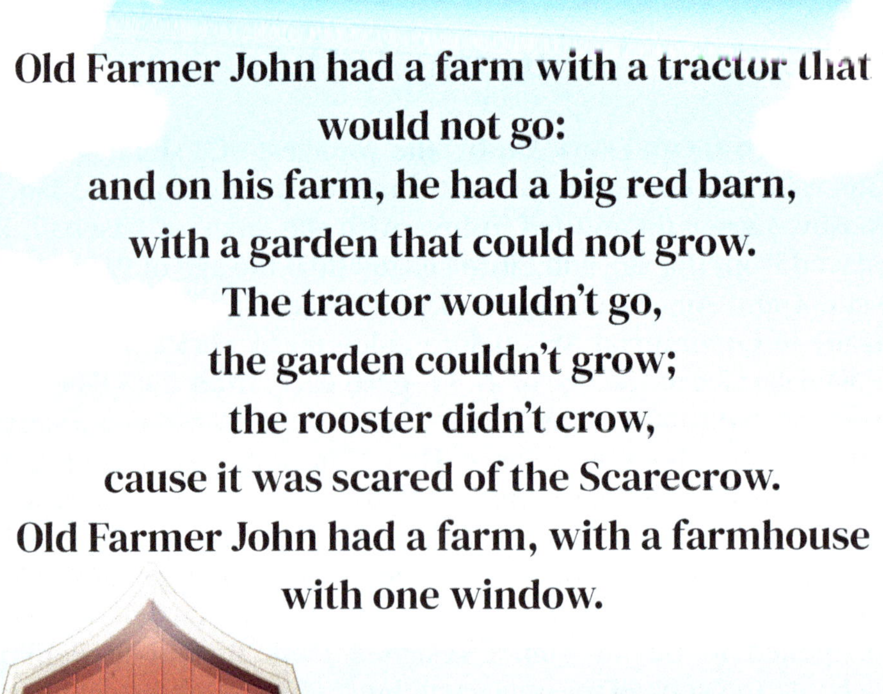

Old Farmer John had a farm with a tractor that
would not go:
and on his farm, he had a big red barn,
with a garden that could not grow.
The tractor wouldn't go,
the garden couldn't grow;
the rooster didn't crow,
cause it was scared of the Scarecrow.
Old Farmer John had a farm, with a farmhouse
with one window.

Old Farmer John had a farm,
with so many animals he loved so;
and on his farm, he didn't give a darn
wherever that his animals would go.
There was a chick chick over here,
a chick chick over there;
a pig in the mud, and a pig who didn't care.
Old Farmer John had a farm, with a farmhouse
with one window.

Old Farmer John had a farm,
with other animals, he did not know;
and on his farm, he would try to stay calm,
when these other animals would put on a show.
The owls would who,
so the other birds would, too;
none of them were in cages,
but they belonged in a zoo.
Old Farmer John had a farm, with a farmhouse with
one window.

Old Farmer John had a farm,
with no wife to let him know;
that on his farm, these animals were all wrong,
and that he should let them go.
He had a cow that couldn't moo,
rooster couldn't cock-a-doodle-doo;
a frog that couldn't hop,
a pig that didn't like slop.
Old Farmer John had a farm, with a farmhouse
with one window.

Old Farmer John had a farm,
with no kids to love him so;
so on his farm, he always stayed alarmed
of the wild animals, not knowing which ones
were foe.
He had a snake that couldn't hiss,
an alligator who hated fish;
a monkey who couldn't climb,
and a zebra with little lines.
Old Farmer John had a farm, with a
farmhouse with one window.

Old Farmer John had a farm,
but his farm was being foreclosed;
because on his farm, there was plenty of harm,
and that all his animals had to go.
There was a sheep who couldn't sleep,
a little lamb that couldn't bleat;
an elephant, a rhino,
a lion that wouldn't eat.
Old Farmer John had a farm, with a farmhouse
with one window.

Old Farmer John had a farm,
but he was a little slow;
because on his farm, he would sing a song,
called eenie meenie minie moe.
He had a pony who was lonely,
a fox who ate macaroni;
a porcupine, a panda,
a sloth that wore sandals.
Old Farmer John had a farm, with a farmhouse
with one window.

Old Farmer John had a farm,
down at the end of the road;
and on his farm was a creek so long
but he didn't even have a boat.
He had a giraffe,
who didn't like to take baths;
butterflies in the skies,
that made you want to laugh.
Old Farmer John had a farm, with a farmhouse
with one window.

Old Farmer John had a farm,
Singing eenie meenie minie moe
the tractor wouldn't go,
the garden couldn't grow,
the rooster didn't crow,
cause it was scared of the Scarecrow.

There was a chick chick over here,
a chick chick over there,
a pig in the mud,
a pig who didn't care,
the owls would who,
the other birds would, too,
none of them were in cages,
they belonged in a zoo.

A cow couldn't moo,
rooster couldn't cock-a- doodle-doo.
a frog that couldn't hop,
a pig that didn't like slop,
a snake that couldn't hiss,
an alligator who hated fish,
a monkey who couldn't climb,
a zebra with little lines.

A sheep who couldn't sleep,
a lamb that couldn't bleat,
an elephant, a rhino,
a lion that wouldn't eat.
a pony who was lonely,
a fox who ate macaroni,
a porcupine, a panda,
a sloth who wore sandals.

He had a giraffe,
who didn't like to take baths,
butterflies in the skies,
that made you want to laugh.
Old Farmer John had a farm,
with a farmhouse with one window.

Old Farmer John had a farm
with a tractor that would not go.
Old Farmer John had a farm,
With so many animals that he loved so.
Old Farmer John had a farm
with other animals he did not know.
Old Farmer John had a farm with no wife
to let him know.

Old Farmer John had a farm,
with no kids to love him so.
Old Farmer John had a farm,
But his farm was being foreclosed.
Old Farmer John had a farm,
But he was a little slow.
Old Farmer John had a farm,
down at the end of the road.
Old Farmer John had a farm,
With a farmhouse with one window.

The End

www.ingramcontent.com/pod-product-compliance
Lightning Source LLC
Chambersburg PA
CBHW070619310726
48982CB00001B/127